SNAFFLES

Written By:
STEPHEN COSGROVE

Illustrated By:
ROBIN JAMES

A Serendipity Book

Dedicated to John Bacon, the inspiration
and perspiration for Snaffles.

Stephen

Many, many years ago, beyond tomorrow and today, was a place of rough and tumble things called the land of Grimm. There were no simple trees and flowers there, only cactus, weeds and rocks. And, oh, how the wind blew!

There weren't many creatures living in this land of Grimm. Oh, maybe you'd find a couple of bedraggled jack rabbits hopping around and nibbling on whatever bits of grass they could find. Or if you looked hard enough, you might even see some rumpled rats scurrying from rock to rock, searching for someplace to hide from the driving wind and dust.

Other than that there were very few creatures who would even want to live there. Very few, that is, save for some purplish colored birds called Gruffs. They were big and rough, with their feathers all matted down with dust from working in the dirt all the time. They had great big eyes that never, ever smiled, and for as long as there had been Gruffs, not one had ever shed a tear or shared laughter with a friend.

Not only did they want to live in the land of Grimm, they loved to live there for they were a motley flock of birds.

Of all the Gruffs that lived in Grimm, only one had even an ounce of emotion. That was a special Gruff called Snaffles.

Snaffles worked just as hard as the other Gruffs, gathering sticks to build new nests. But occasionally, he would get just a little curious, something the other Gruffs really frowned upon. He'd work really hard from sun-up to sun-down, breaking sticks to make smaller sticks, but sometimes he'd just stop and ask "Why?"

Usually one of the other Gruffs would turn, scowl at Snaffles, and with feathers flying, cuff him alongside the head and tell him to get back to work.

One day, while Snaffles was out looking for broken branches and twigs, he heard the strangest sound he'd ever heard. He looked around carefully but couldn't see anything. Then, he heard it again! He sneaked over, as quietly as he could sneak, and peeked over the edge of a big rock.

There, right in front of him, was the strangest sight he had ever seen: a long-eared, scruffy-looking rabbit, rolling around from side to side, making the most ridiculous noises Snaffles had ever heard. "What are you doing?" he asked as gruffly as he could.

The rabbit looked up in surprise and said, "I'm laughing." And then with a giggle and a gulp, he rolled from side to side in uncontrolled laughter.

Snaffles scrunched up his beak and asked sheepishly, "Uh, what's laughing?"

With that the rabbit laughed even harder. It must have been two or three minutes before he could control himself long enough to answer. "Laughing is one way to show you're happy," he chuckled.

Snaffles thought for a moment feeling really dumb and then said: "What's happy?"

"Well I'll be! I bet you don't even know what emotions are, do you?"

Snaffles swished his foot around in the dirt and shook his head, "No."

"There are all kinds of emotions," the rabbit explained. "There is sad . . ." and he tried to look really sad, ". . . and there is mad . . ." and the rabbit looked really mad, almost scaring poor Snaffles, ". . . and there is happy," and he began to laugh and laugh.

Snaffles scratched his head and said, "That looks easy enough." And with that, he began to try with all of his might. He twisted his face into a million different contortions, trying to look happy, but the best he could do was look awfully silly, which made the rabbit laugh even harder.

"You dumb old rabbit! You don't even know what you're talking about. I'll go ask the other Gruffs; they'll know what all these emotion things are."

He turned abruptly on his heel and flew back to the Gruff nest, leaving the rabbit rolling on the ground just as he had been found.

Snaffles shuffled right up to the boss of all the Gruffs. "Uh, excuse me sir, but what are emotions?" he asked in his most respectful voice.

The boss Gruff looked at him and then said roughly, "What you want to know that for, boy?"

"Well, uh, you see, I met this rabbit and he told me about being mad, and happy, and sad; only when I tried to do them, nothing happened."

"Best you don't find out," the boss Gruff said sternly as he ruffled his feathers. "Because only babies and sissies show emotions. Now get your feathery hide back to work before I bust your head with this stick!" And he turned back to his work.

Snaffles didn't know what to do. He knew the boss Gruff would never lie to him but at the same time the rabbit had no reason to lie either.

"I know what I'll do," he thought. "I'll try to find my own emotions. Without help from the other Gruffs or that stupid rabbit."

And try he did. He looked under rocks, and behind cactus. He even looked under an old lizard that happened by, but the only thing he found was dust, dirt, and some old sticks. To make matters worse, no matter where he looked, he could hear the rabbit's laughter ringing in his ears. Finally, out of frustration, he shouted, "Okay, rabbit, if you're so smart then you show me where I can find emotions!"

Like magic, the rabbit popped up from behind a rock. "Come on, Gruff," he giggled, "follow me and I'll show you where to find emotions." Without waiting for an answer, the rabbit began hopping away. A very confused Snaffles shuffled right behind.

They hopped and shuffled for many a mile on a very old and well-worn path and finally climbed a hill that overlooked the most beautiful crystal pond that Snaffles had ever seen. "This," said the rabbit, "is the Pool of Forgotten Tears."

"Well, what am I supposed to do now?" Snaffles grumbled.

"Go to the water and drink," smiled the rabbit as he nibbled on one of his ears. "I think your thirst will be satisfied."

"Dumb rabbit!" muttered Snaffles. "This doesn't look like an answer to me. But I am thirsty and the water sure looks good." He ambled down to the pond, waded into the water and drank deeply. As he was finishing his second drink. Snaffles happened to see his own reflection in the pond and started feeling strange all over. Then, ever so slowly, tears began to slip from his eyes and down his beak, splashing into the water below.

"Oh no!" sobbed Snaffles, "Now water is falling from my eyes."

"That's alright," consoled the rabbit. "Those are only tears. They won't hurt you."

"Tears!" wailed a saddened Snaffles. "I can't cry. Only babies and sissies cry. You cheated me, rabbit. I wanted to find my emotions and learn how to laugh and all you gave me was tears."

"No, Snaffles," chuckled the rabbit, "I didn't cheat you. You can't find happiness until you know sadness and you can't have true laughter until you know the taste of your own tears. Look deeper into the water, there is more."

Sure enough, Snaffles gazed into the water and, for the first time, saw before him a dirty, feathery face with tears tracing a dusty line down his cheeks. He looked funny, and the longer he looked the funnier he looked. Then, from deep, deep inside himself came a happy rumbling laughter that spilled out and rolled over the countryside.

Snaffles and the rabbit laughed and cried for nearly a day. They laughed at the clouds as they skipped across the sky and they cried when a cricket died.

Finally Snaffles said, "I must take emotions back to the other Gruffs. Help me find a bucket to carry some water from the Pool of Forgotten Tears." They searched about and found a hollowed old piece of cactus and filled it with water.

Then, ever so carefully, they headed back to the Gruff's camp, laughing and giggling all the way.

When they arrived, Snaffles called all the Gruffs together and told them what had happened. But, they didn't believe him.

"That sounds like a bunch of bunk!" said the boss of all the Gruffs. "Now everybody get back to work!"

"Wait!" shouted Snaffles. "If you don't believe me, then take a drink of the water before you leave."

They all thought for a moment. Then the boss Gruff stomped over, grabbed the hollow cactus, dipped his beak into it and took a big drink. One by one the other Gruffs drank too. When everyone had finished, the boss looked around and said, "See. Nothing happened. Come on Gruffs, back to work!" And they all began shuffling back to their jobs.

"Don't worry," said the rabbit to a saddened Snaffles, "it will work. It will just take some time." Then, after poking Snaffles in the wing, he said, "Come with me and I'll show you the funniest cactus in the whole desert." With a giggle and a grin, Snaffles and the rabbit skipped away.

And if you listened very carefully, amidst the noise of breaking sticks, you could hear the muffled laughter in the land of Grimm.

So if someone is crying
Or laughter you do hear
Remember a Gruff named Snaffles
And the Pool of Forgotten Tears.